# THE DRAGON STONE

Vadia Rademaker

authorHOUSE®

AuthorHouse™ UK Ltd.
500 Avebury Boulevard
Central Milton Keynes, MK9 2BE
www.authorhouse.co.uk
Phone: 08001974150

First published by AuthorHouse 7/16/2010

ISBN: 978-1-4490-3796-3 (sc)

This book is printed on acid-free paper.

# CHAPTER 1

## The Move

26 Elm Park looked like a very ordinary house from the outside. Mum and dad had bought it because it was big and the price was right. We moved in during the summer holidays and that was when our adventures began!

Entrance to the house was gained through the back garden because it was too far to walk around to the front of the house. Mum liked to call it our back-to-front house.

The garden in the back was a mess when I first saw it but mum in her usual cheery way was delighted; "A blank canvas, just think what we can create!"

When dad opened the door, my heart skipped a beat. It was the first time I had laid eyes on the house. The lounge had been stripped bare of all paint and wallpaper. 'Ugh!' I thought, now I know why my parents had said they had got it at a good price, no-one else would have wanted to buy it! With a pounding heart full of dread I

1

climbed the stairs to the first floor where my bedroom was apparently situated. I was dreading what I would find!

My room had been painted a bright cheery yellow and on the floor was a cream coloured carpet. It was the kind that as you stepped onto it, you would sink into. The kind of carpet you dreamed of owning one day. I heaved a sigh of relief. At least this was one room that was in good order and it would be mine!

Mum and dad's bedroom would be on the top floor, which meant I had a whole floor to myself! I decided that I would enjoy living here and started to make plans to decorate my floor!

From the moment we moved in the house seemed to take on a life and personality of it's own and if I did not live there at the time I think I would have dismissed this story as another one of mum's fanciful tales.

What our neighbours thought of all this, I still do not know, but am tempted to ask them one day in the not so distant future.

# The First Night

'BANG, THUMP, CRASH,' Mum came running down the top flight of stairs with her nightgown billowing behind her. "Was that you?" she gasped as she raced into my room.

"Noooo, I don't think so," I replied shakily and then we heard it again; only this time it was a lot louder and seemed to be coming from the walls of the house.

"That does it! I'm going to see what is happening!" and with a swirl of her nightgown she charged out of my bedroom, down the next flight of stairs.

"Oh, my," we heard mum gasp from below.

Curiosity got the better of dad and I as we both hurtled downstairs, switching on lights as we descended into the dark.

Sitting on the kitchen floor, in a ring of lights was mum.

She was talking to a small ragged, strangely dressed, saucer eyed being. He was about 4ft tall and appeared to have a hunched back. His hands and feet were frog like with what looked like suckers on the palms and soles of his feet. His face had the look of a startled deer and from his chin there grew a very long white beard.

"Meet Bling," smiled mum as we stood in the kitchen and gaped at the strange creature.

Bling was a changeling. He lived at the bottom of the garden, deep in the ground under the nut tree or so he said, and he needed mum's help.

3

"The changes in Freeland happened gradually," explained Bling, "in fact it was so gradual that we didn't notice it at first, but then things started to get very topsy turvy, and by then it was almost too late!"

It was at this point that Bling started to sob and as his crystal tears dripped off the end of his huge nose pools of light flooded the kitchen floor. These were the lights we had found mum sitting in the middle of.

"Oh dear, oh dear, how can I help?" enquired mum in hushed tones; a sound not often associated with mum who normally had a loud booming voice.

"Well," sniffed a much relieved Bling, "I would like to hold you to the terms of our agreement."

"What agreement is that?" asked my startled father, who was only now starting to comprehend that Bling was not a burglar but a very disgruntled little person with loads of problems that he wanted to share with us.

"Oh, an agreement that I made when I was about Vickys age, to come to the assistance of any Freeland folk who had need of my help," replied mum almost dreamily to a very stunned audience; casting her mind back to when she had first met the Freelanders at the bottom of a garden. She had accidentally fallen into a pond and the Freelanders had agreed to help her out on condition that if they ever needed help she would be willing to assist in any way that she could. Desperate to climb out of the very mucky pond and thinking that she could never help these magical creatures, mum instantly agreed. Mum had almost forgotten about it, and now the time had finally arrived!

"We're wasting time, and I can't stay out too long or the Drogonians will know that I've managed to escape and contact you," resumed Bling who was now sitting next to mum and pulling at his beard which was tangled with what appeared to be old leaves and decaying wood!

"I'm not sure I know what you expect from me," said a bemused mum, "I certainly don't possess any special powers and if you are struggling to deal with these Drogonians yourselves I don't know what I can do."

"It is important that we enlist your help Rose, because the Drogonians are coming to your world next," said Bling, "Let me explain to you what has already happened!"

# Bling's Tale

"The Drogonians have already managed to infiltrate the upper levels of earth and have developed a system of mind control to get certain humans to do what they want. Using these folk the Drogonians are slowly and successfully infiltrating into your world, and if we do not stop them all will be lost not only in our world but in yours as well," stammered Bling.

"Drogonians? But who are these Drogonians?" questioned dad putting the kettle on to make us all a cup of tea; a ritual that he always did at the first sign of trouble or upset.

Bling appeared to be slightly irritated at this intrusion and gave dad an irritable "Humph! I would like to continue if you don't mind! No more interruptions if you please!"

"Long, long ago, when the world first began there were two brothers. The two brothers were very competitive and were always challenging each other. To make their battles more interesting; each brother began to create an army of different folk and beings. These creatures were made to do the brothers bidding until eventually; through loyal service they were given 'wills' of their own.

The eldest brother created the Drogonians in order to infiltrate and read the minds of his younger brother's army; who were under strict orders to love and protect all of the fantasy folk. At first the Drogonians failed in their attempts, as they had to report all their intentions to the oldest brother and often these messengers were intercepted and persuaded to return without harm to themselves or others; but as time marched on and the Drogonians gained free will, there was less and less need for them to report back to their creator and some of them started to develop war tactics hitherto unknown.

New leaders emerged and the strongest of these leaders has survived even to this day. This was the beginning of the Drogonian colonies," sighed Bling.

"The colonies have grown a lot since then and their leaders are far more ambitious than they were a long time ago. Why; I heard a report just the other day saying that hundreds were already on their way to the top to join the newly established mind control units."

"Right, I've heard enough" said mum in her usual business like manner," I'm going to get a change of clothing and while I'm getting ready I want Vicky (that's me!) to pack me a bag with hiking gear, a flash light and Frank can make me a thermos flask of his famous tea to take with on the journey!"

Mum raced up the stairs two at a time and grabbed a pair of jeans, a T-shirt and an old cardigan that she liked to wear around the house. She called it her comfort cardigan and I guess she would need all the comfort that she could get!

"Can we go with you?" asked Frank. I think we were both dreaming about the exciting adventure mum was about to embark on!
"We are going to need someone to stay in the house, in case we need to get help quickly", said Rose and Bling almost in unison and then they left.

# Operation Nut Tree

Bling and Rose made their way quietly to the bottom of the garden where the nut tree grew. It was under this nut tree that Bling had said he lived. Dad and I watched mum; who towered over the little changeling bend down and speak to him in a hushed whisper.

"Oh no" said Vicky turning to Frank, "I forgot to pack the thermos flask of tea into mum's knap sack".

"Perhaps if you hurry, you will be able to catch her before she begins her descent," said an anxious Frank who believed that tea was the answer to all life's problems.

"Bling, I need you to start the descent without me. I'll follow shortly because I need to ensure the rope is tightly secured, otherwise I will have no way of getting back once our rescue mission is over," said Rose, whilst coiling the rope that Frank had put into her knap sack, around the trunk of the tree.

Under cover of darkness; with the use of his very sticky hands and feet; Bling began the descent effortlessly and noiselessly. He scraped his knee occasionally on the rough bark but was very careful to keep his mutterings under his breath just in case the Drogonians were listening.

Rose was an expert at knot tying; she and Vicky had learnt all about rope tying from Frank who had spent a long time in the navy. Finally the last knot was slipped into place and Rose began her journey into the great unknown.

The inside walls of the tree felt hard and sharp. Rose looked up and noticed what appeared to be foothold cuts that had been made in the trunk. Quick as a wink, she started to feel around in the dark for more footholds; she found what she was looking for and used them to make her descent easier.

"Ouch", snarled Bling, "you want to be more careful with those feet of yours."

" Oops, sorry Bling, I thought that you would have been much further down the tree by now," giggled Rose.

"Oh that's easy for you to say," grumbled Bling, "you got ropes and footholds."

"Why don't you use the footholds?" asked a puzzled Rose.

"What; and not use me hands and feet in the way they was intended! I think not!" spluttered a very indignant Bling.

'THUD.'

"What was that?" asked Rose feeling for the next foothold.

"Me, I've reached the bottom sooner then I thinked!" answered a very disgruntled Bling.

As soon as Rose got to the bottom of the tree she noticed a green door with two buttons next to it.

"What are these buttons and this door?" asked Rose, in surprise.

"We call it a trunkulator, and it pretty much works like an elevator up top," stated a proud and knowledgeable Bling.

"What! Do you mean I could have taken a trunkulator from the top of the tree above ground to the bottom!" spluttered Rose angrily. "Why didn't you tell me? No more surprises please Bling, we need to do this as quickly and as quietly as possible and if that means doing it without fuss and not using our appendages the way nature intended us to, we will! Do you understand?"

Bling blinked in the half-light of the trunkulator, gulped and nodded that he understood.

"But," he said, almost as an after thought "If you had used the trunkulator to come down in, you would not have the rope tied to the top level."

"Why Bling, you're absolutely right! I had not thought of that. What a clever thing to say! Please accept my apology."

Bling smiled in the half-light of the nut tree. Nobody had ever apologised to him before and it felt good.

# CHAPTER TWO

## Vicky Joins The Fight

Once Rose had gotten over her annoyance with Bling, she began to look around. She found herself in a rather curious room filled with the smell of ripe and roasting nuts. The smell made her hungry, but she knew that there would be no time to eat, and besides her family was waiting for her above ground.

Suddenly the lights of the trunkulator started to Blink.

"Quick, we must hide," shouted a terrified Bling.

"But how and where?" cried Rose, who was beginning to understand that she was not as brave as she had made her family think she was!

"Turn yourself invisible like this!" screamed Bling, who suddenly disappeared.

"Thanks a lot Bling," Rose groaned as the doors to the trunkulator slowly opened.

Inside stood Vicky holding a thermos flask of herbal tea! "Vicky, what on earth are you doing here?" gasped Rose.

Vicky stepped out of the trunkulator, looked at Rose and said, "Who are you and how do you know my name?"

"Maybe your eyes still need to adjust to the light – can't you see it's me, mum," exclaimed Rose.

Vicky stood still for what seemed like ages carefully looking Rose up and down.

Bling had decided to become visible again and was watching the interchange with great curiosity. "Wow, this light must really be strange, cos you don't look anything like mum," stammered a surprised Vicky.

"What on earth do you mean?" asked Rose, stepping up to the trunkulator to catch a glimpse of herself in the mirrored walls.

Reflected from the mirrors stood a tiny nymph. She had dark short-cropped hair, tiny, delicate wings, milky white skin and huge luminous eyes. Her jeans and T-shirt had been transformed into a soft, silken, turquoise dress that hung in loose folds around her bare legs. As Rose gazed at her reflection, her luminous eyes became larger and started to fill with tears.

"Oh dear Bling, is this another one of your tricks?"

"Don't cry mum, you're the most beautiful creature I have ever seen!" said Vicky trying to comfort her mum but not realising that she was also beginning to change into an almost exact replica of her mum.

"Everybody changes when they steps inside the nut tree," said an indignant Bling, "I had nothing to do with it!"

"But why haven't you changed Bling," asked a curious Vicky still unaware of her own changes.

"Because I have been down here so long, it would take a very long time for me to change into my above ground shape, so I guess I just stay the same no matter where I is or been," sighed Bling.

It was at this point that Rose noticed that Vicky had also changed into a wood nymph!

"Ooooh Vicky, you have grown a pair of wings as well", whispered Rose.

Both Rose and Vicky watched in silence and amazement, as they metamorphed into their underworld bodies. Vicky stood admiring her wings while Rose examined the pointy shape of her ears.

# The Adventures Begin

"Rose, Vicky, quick this way before we are seen," urged an anxious Bling. He could not understand their fascination with their reflections in the mirror of the trunkulator.

The two nymphs followed the strange frog like creature they had come to know as Bling out of the base of the nut tree. An unusual and strange world awaited them. The sun appeared to have risen, but had not quite made it all the way up into the sky. The trees, of which there appeared to be a large variety, had all shed their leaves and stood shivering in the early morning light. In the distance a family of foxes, or something similar were frolicking amongst the fallen leaves, whilst a huge bear looked on.

"Don't let the Drogonian see you," whispered Bling.

"What does he look like", asked a curious and startled Rose and Vicky in unison.

"He's the big creature watching the leaf eaters," answered Bling.

The two curious onlookers stood and watched the leaf eaters for a few more minutes and then Bling hurried them on down into what appeared to be a large tunnel.

"This is Moth Hall," said Bling proudly, "This is where I grew up with my 5 brothers and sisters."

Moth Hall was well lit with artificial lighting in the shape of torches. At the far end of the room stood a huge big chair that had been chained to the floor. On the walls hung tapestries depicting heroes of the past in fine silken skein.

"Mum, look," squealed an excited Vicky, "There is a picture of you on the wall, on a horse with wings!"

"Rose, we need you to contact Firefox so that we can get to the Free Land quickly and without the Drogonians seeing us," said Bling. "We can't stay here too long, because Moth Hall has been taken over by the Drogonian we saw outside. That is his chair and if he finds us in here he will turn us into leaf eaters or something worse!"

"I don't understand," said a puzzled Rose, "if Moth Hall is now in the hands of the enemy, why did you bring us here?"

"So that you could see the tapestries and begin to understand without asking too many questions. Questions will waste time and I need you to be able to have an idea of our previous glory so that you know what it is we are fighting for," said Bling who was close to tears because of the ransacking of Moth Hall. "Not what it used to be, not what it used to be'" he muttered under his breath.

"But how do I summon a horse that I have only seen in a tapestry?"

"Concentrate hard and use your mind. Call his name softly and reveal yourself to him when he asks you to do so," answered Bling.

# The Summoning Of Firefox

Rose closed her eyes and imagined the magnificent red horse she had seen in the tapestry. Using her imagination, she gently whispered Firefox's name. Over and over again she called his name and then suddenly she heard a voice inside her head saying "Reveal yourself to the one that you call, and if you are friend I'll meet you in Moth Hall."

Remembering her reflection and concentrating hard she imagined she was revealing herself to Firefox.

"Wow, that was quick," said Vicky staring at the magnificent fire horse standing in front of them.

Rose opened her eyes to see Firefox looking at her with a great deal of interest.

He was like no other horse she had ever seen. Firefox stood in a blaze of light and was the colour of a warm fire on a cold winter's night. His wings were lifted up in anticipation of the flight they were intending to take.

"Greetings friend, I have come to be of service to you and your allies," he said.

"Thank you great kind creature, we need all the help that we can get," said Rose ever so quietly, that Vicky was not quite sure if she had heard her mother or if she had imagined it.

"Hurry, we need to leave now, before the Great Drogonian gets back from the leaf fields," whispered Bling.

"We shall leave at once," cried Firefox, "get onto my back and hold onto each other so that you do not fall!"

Rose sprang onto Firefox's back with the greatest of ease. She guessed that her wings must have helped her get on more easily. Vicky flew up next and sat behind Rose who held onto Firefox's mane to steady herself. Finally Bling leapt up into the air almost frog like and settled behind Vicky, using his sticky hands and feet to hang on and keep himself from falling.

The great horse leapt up into the air and flew from the Hall. The three friends hung on tightly to each other as they felt the cold wind sweep through their clothes. Rose and Vicky could hear and feel the huge wings beating the air above their heads.

"Open your eyes," yelled a gleeful and excited Bling. "You can see for miles from up here!"

"That's what I'm afraid of", said Vicky with eyes tightly shut.

"Oh Vicky, Bling is right, you can see for miles, open your eyes dear and look. You'll be perfectly safe!"

# The Flight Of Firefox

Slowly and timidly Vicky opened first one eye then the other. She gasped in both awe and delight; far below them was a world that no one knew existed and she was flying above it on a magical fire horse with wings!

"That's where the Drogonian territory ends," indicated Bling pointing, "You can see how the landscape changes. Many years ago all the land looked the same and there was no difference between Drogonian and Free land."

The land below them was empty and almost desolate. The wind had picked up and the trees below were now shivering uncontrollably. The leaf eaters could be seen working in the leaf fields with the huge Drogonian looking on.

"Oh those poor darling leaf eaters," said Rose sadly. "Do they ever stop to rest, or does that beastly Drogonian make them work all day and night?"

Suddenly the Drogonian looked up and gnashed his huge teeth at Firefox!

"He's seen us," yelled a frightened Bling "Oh my, oh my, I wonder if he recognises me?"

"Don't worry Bling; you're miles away from the Drogonian. He won't be able to reach you while you are in the air flying." said Rose kindly.

"What about when I'm not flying? Ooooh, he knows it's me, what am I going to do?" cried a terrified Bling.

"Have some herbal tea Bling, it will make you feel much better!" suggested Vicky.

Rose and Vicky began to giggle. It was a really silly suggestion to offer Bling a cup of Frank's famous herbal tea to take his mind off his troubles, especially when they were flying through the air at a tremendous speed hanging on for dear life!

"Mmmmmph," said Bling glowering at both nymphs.

"Look mum," shouted Vicky "the landscape is different. We have crossed the border between Drogonian and Free Land and look, all the trees have leaves and they are not shivering, but.... wait, what are the trees doing?" she added very puzzled.

"Waving," said Bling.

Firefox was now beginning his descent into the land known to Rose and Vicky as the Free Land. As they approached the landing area they could not help but notice how happy and gay all the plants looked. Both the trees and the grass now appeared to be waving and the flowers were bobbing their heads up and down in unison.

"Oh my look," gasped Rose in awe, "it seems all the Free Landers have come to meet us!"

# The Freelanders

"Greetings Salome, these are my friends who have come a long way from the top of the nut tree to assist us in our quest against the Drogonians", said Firefox as he executed a gentle landing.

In front of the tall fire horse stood a most unusual looking girl. On her head were what seemed like the horns of a dragon. Her soft milky skin had the markings of a lithesome cheetah and her wings when opened were almost bat like in their appearance. She gazed at the small group seated in front of her with penetrating azure eyes.

"I am Salome, keeper of secrets, and whom do I now address?" she asked in a soft almost hypnotic voice.

"Bling, here, guardian of; of water," answered Bling hurriedly while looking around nervously at the assembled Freelanders.

Never before had Bling seen so many Freelanders assembled together. They were normally solitary folk who went about their own business.

"I know who you are Bling and what the nature of your business is!" said Salome caustically, "It is the new comers that I address!"

Rose looked into the eyes of Salome. She could feel herself been drawn into Salome's stare and found that she could not resist. It was then that Rose understood Salome was just been polite and already knew who they were and what their business was.

" I am Rose from 26 Elm Park Close and this is my daughter Vicky who has accompanied me," she answered politely.

Vicky was glad that her mum had introduced her and that she was sitting behind her mum on the fire horse because she was not sure that she would be able to speak. Her mouth felt dry and she felt a rushing of wind in her private thoughts, which made her feel very uncomfortable. She guessed that Salome was probing her thoughts for all her hidden secrets and did not like it!

"Enough Salome, it is time to take our visitors to the king's chambers, release them!" admonished a stern voice.

A dragon like creature with an enormous expanse of wing and a kindly face stood behind Salome. It was this creature that had spoken.

"Come," he said kindly to the new comers, " we need to continue our journey to the Freelander Citadel in order to get there before the sun sets."

# CHAPTER THREE

## The Freeland Citadel

Fire horse and dragon leapt into the air almost simultaneously. The beating of their wings created a giant whirlwind on the ground. Trees bent over to avoid been snapped into firewood and Freelanders could be seen diving for cover under the bowed branches for protection.

Perching on the back of the dragon, Salome instructed Firefox to follow them to the Citadel. The girl looked very comfortable seated on the back of the giant dragon and he in turn looked happy to have her seated there.

"Who is the dragon and what is he called," asked Vicky.

"He is Fidel, protector of truth. He and Salome are inseparable. They have been together since the beginning of time," said Firefox.

Rose and Vicky did not speak for the rest of the journey. They were both trying hard to concentrate on the landscape below so that they would be able to describe it to Frank who was waiting at home for them.

Far below them they could see endless forests of trees and gentle rolling hills. A silvery blue river meandered its way lazily through the landscape, making its way towards the sea.

They were now flying high above the clouds and could see the sun making its way steadily downward.

"Almost time for the sun to set," whinnied Firefox, "We need to press on more quickly than before."

The three riders thought they had been flying fast up until then but soon realised that Firefox had definitely not been flying at his optimum speed. With a sudden jerk, they found themselves hurtling toward the Citadel at breakneck speed!

Rose could feel the wind pressing urgently against her and it was at this point she imagined what an astronaut must feel like when he experiences the G forces pressed against him in a bid to break gravity and enter into space. It was not a feeling she liked and she wondered how Vicky and Bling were managing.

The turrets of the Citadel could be seen rising above the clouds. They glowed golden in the sinking sunlight. All felt a sense of relief when Firefox reigned in his supersonic speed and began to drop from the sky very quickly. He was gliding towards the immense outer gate that was the entrance to the Citadel.

# Meeting The King

"Halt who goes there!" demanded Valour sentinel of the Citadel and guardian of the Golden Gates of Freeland.

Valour was divinely beautiful. She had long red hair; a delicate porcelain skin and she appeared to be over 6ft tall. She was clothed in fine silk, which fitted her like a glove. On her feet she wore black leather boots that ended at her knees. At her side she wore an enormous sword sheathed in gold.

Valour knew that the two strangers astride Firefox, accompanied by Salome and Fidel the Dragon must be allies, for Salome and Fidel would never have brought them this far into the kingdom if they had posed any kind of a threat to the king; but Valour enjoyed showing off her superb swordsmanship. Finally, after what seemed like ages and tiring of the demonstration, Valour sheathed her sword, turned on her heals and instructed the party to follow her.

Rose and Vicky gasped as they saw what lay behind the Golden Gates of the Citadel. In front of them was a huge tripod cast out of precious metal and stones. The three 'legs' of the tripod were in the shape of horse heads and resting between the three heads, balanced with precision just behind their ears was the.... sun!

"Greetings friends, I have been awaiting your arrival", said a warm friendly voice.

Standing next to the tripod, barely visible because of the brilliance of the sun stood a tall man dressed in a white flowing robe. "I am King Luthian, summoner of light, welcome to the Golden Citadel, home of the light bringer."

Rose felt timid and awed by this great king who had been expecting their arrival and found herself fumbling to get down from her perch on top of Firefox. She climbed down as quickly as she could followed by Vicky and Bling. The three of them bowed silently in unison.

"Come," said the King in a gentle voice, "we have no time for extreme formalities, and we need to get started immediately!"

King Luthian led them into the Citadel, where a banquet beyond Rose and Vickys' wildest imagination lay spread on an enormous table.

"Eat first and then we will talk."

All three of them felt very hungry. It had been a long time since Bling had eaten his last meal and he did not need a second invitation to start helping himself to the food that was on the table.

Every food imaginable appeared to be on the table and as if by magic whatever they felt they might like to eat materialized on their plates!

"Wow, I'd love a table like this at home," marvelled Rose as she tucked into the food that had appeared on her plate.

"Beats cooking," agreed Vicky with a mouthful of succulent, ripe seedless grapes.

# Bestowing Of Power

The banquet had been wonderful. Rose had eaten more than usual and agreed with Vicky when she declared that it was the best tasting food they had ever had.

"It is time for the bestowing of powers," declared King Luthian.

It seemed that everybody in Freeland had special powers and now King Luthian was ready to bestow special powers on Rose and Vicky. The two nymphs looked very much alike and it was hard to keep track of who was who, or so Bling thought. He was eager to be able to tell the difference between the two and felt that the bestowing of power would help him in this.

"First, to get her powers will be Vicky," said King Luthian, which shocked Rose a little as she thought she would be the first one to receive a power because she was the oldest, but then she remembered that age meant nothing in Freeland as most people had been born a long time ago any way!

"Vicky will receive the power of the crystal dragon," stated King Luthian and with a huge wave of his arm; pointed at Vicky, who was waiting expectantly. A fiery blast emitted from the kings fingertips and surrounded the girl. She did not know what to expect but nothing had prepared her for the hot blast of magic that encircled her and then settled in her hair, nose, mouth, arms and legs!

A tingly sensation ran down her back to her toes. She tried to lift her arm and look at herself to see what this strange magic was doing. Then she gasped in horror!

"I can't see myself", she screamed!

"You have the power of the crystal dragon. You can cloak yourself in invisibility and you can create crystal bubbles from the back of your throat when you are in dragon mode for others to hide inside so they too may be cloaked in invisibility when they travel," stated King Luthian.

"Now it is Rose's turn," he said pointing towards Rose.

"You shall have the power of the red dragon, keeper of time and summoner of the elements," he declared as a huge thunderbolt leapt from his hand and shot like an arrow towards Rose. The arrow like missile hit her in the middle of her chest and she felt a warm sensation flooding through her entire body. After a while she started to feel extremely light headed and was sure she was about to faint when through the hazy mist she caught sight of an hourglass.

"Take hold of the hour glass Rose and guard it with your life," smiled the king, "come I must now show you both how to use your newly acquired powers so that you can use them formidably against the enemy."

## Vicky's Lesson Begins

Vicky was taken by the hand and led away from the banquet hall. She found herself following a dwarf dressed in a velveteen suit the colour of daffodils in the springtime. He was surprisingly quick for his seemingly vast age and short stature and Vicky found it extremely difficult to keep up with him.

"Wait up, please," groaned Vicky who wanted to do a bit of sight seeing on the way to where ever they were headed.

"No time for looking around now lass, there will be plenty of time for that later!" said the disgruntled dwarf who by now had crossed the sun courtyard and had entered another room that appeared to be devoid of all furniture.

"Where are we?" asked a surprised Vicky who had expected this room to be just as grandly furnished as the one they had left.

"We are in the training room," said the dwarf, "and the reason the room is bare is because we don't want you destroying nothing while you learn how to control the powers whats been given to you."

Vicky shuddered in the cold dark room and was eager to begin her lessons so that she could leave, but not before the dwarf  could see she had learnt to control her newly acquired powers.

"Now to begin with......you need to learn how to metamorphose into your dragon shape before you can become invisible and blow bubbles," said the dwarf tutor.

"But I became invisible in the banquet hall without met…, met…, metamorphosing into a dragon first," Vicky pointed out.

"That's because his magic was still on you," explained the impatient dwarf, "now you needs to be quiet and pay attention so's that you can learn something," he added with annoyance.
"Hold your breath for a few minutes, until you find it very difficult to breathe, then without letting your breath out, take another deep breath and then you should be able to feel yourself begin to change," he ordered.

Vicky obediently followed her tutor's instructions, but found it extremely difficult to take another breath, when all she wanted to do was let go of the breath that she had been holding.

"I can't," she said simply, "I thought I could, but I can't"

"Try again, or you'll never get it right, and if you don't get it right you have to keep on trying!" Said the now red in the face impatient little dwarf.

"Stop yelling at me!" screamed Vicky, "I'd like to see you try and do it if you think it's so easy," she added for good measure.

"Right, then I'll show you missy!" shouted the dwarf who proceeded to take a great big gulp of air, hold his breath for a few minutes, but when he tried to take a second breath there was a huge big explosion of air that forced it's way out of his lungs and into his mouth!

Vicky who had always been taught to be polite and show good manners knew that it was wrong to laugh at others but could not help herself. She let out a loud guffaw and rolled onto the floor in peals of laughter.

"Oh Mr. Dwarf, you should have seen your face!" squealed a delighted Vicky.

"Humph," said the now chastised teacher, "lets try again."

Vicky found him to be much kinder since he had tried to hold his breath and had failed in his attempt. He treated her in a gentler fashion and encouraged her to continue trying every time she failed. After several attempts Vicky began to feel extremely dizzy and light headed! She felt that she could not continue when suddenly she heard the dwarf cry,

"Eureka, you have done it Vicky, you have metamorphosed into your dragon form!"

Vicky bowed her head and looked down at herself. Instead of the body of a wood nymph she had that of a dragon! A crystal dragon!

"Now, start to blow bubbles using the back of your throat," said the dwarf gleefully.

Blowing bubbles was easier than metamorphosing and Vicky quickly got the knack of it. She started to feel adventurous and experimented with different sized bubbles. Each bubble appeared to be more beautiful than the last and then it was time to stop.

"You have done well, I wonder how Rose has fared with her lessons? Let's go and find out!"

Vicky was thrilled and could hardly wait to return to the banquet hall to show off her new found powers to her mother. She was also eager to find out about her mum's powers and how her mum had fared in her lessons.

# Rose Finds Out About Dragons

Rose had watched Vicky leave the banquet hall with the comically dressed dwarf. She was concerned that Vicky's short temper would land her in a bit of hot water but King Luthian assured her that Magpop the dwarf could handle any situation he found himself in. "In fact," said King Luthian smiling, "Magpop has a bit of a short fuse himself!"

"Oh dear," asked Rose worriedly, "do you think it was wise to pair the two of them together?"
King Luthian laughed and laughed and then he said, "That is exactly why I chose Magpop to be Vicky's tutor," adding with a twinkle in his eye, "I think they will both learn from this experience!"

Then King Luthian changed the subject abruptly and asked "What do you know about dragons Rose?" asked
"Not an awful lot," admitted Rose, who really didn't know anything about dragons, but didn't want to say so.

" I am going to give you a gift," said King Luthian solemnly. "It is not a gift to be taken lightly, nor can it ever be given away and it must be guarded with your life. You are to keep it on your person at all times so that no-one can ever rob you of it!" he added.

King Luthian clapped his hands and as if by magic a tiny dog, walking on his back legs, entered the hall carrying a small box crafted in gold and silver. From where she was standing Rose could see that the box was very old. From where she stood she could make out various magical signs and symbols that had been engraved into the lid of the box, which King Luthian was now opening using a key that he had taken from the folds of his robe. As soon as the key slid into the lock, the lid sprang open to reveal the treasure within!

"Oh my," gasped Rose as she looked inside the box, " that is the most beautiful ring that I have ever seen!"

Inside the box, nestled on black velvet was a gold ring with a magnificent stone. The stone seemed to be changing colours as if by magic, but on closer inspection Rose saw that it did not change colours at all, it was all the colours at once!

The colours appeared to change depending on how the light reflected off of it.

"This is the Dragon Stone ring," said King Luthian, "It is the only Dragon Stone in the world. Many will envy you this ring, so you must never take it off."

"But what is the Dragon Stone?" asked Rose further examining the ring from a respectable distance.

"A Dragon stone is the most precious stone in the entire world. It was taken from the head of the father of all dragons upon his death and it holds all the collective memories and secrets of all dragons that have ever existed or yet to come. The stone will assist the person who wears it, by revealing all present, past and forgotten dragon lore."

"But how?" asked Rose still very puzzled and intrigued by the ring.

"By wearing it," said Luthian.

King Luthian took the Dragon Stone out of its enchanted box and carefully placed it onto Rose's left ring finger. Rose felt it slide on and then as if by magic adjust to her correct finger size! She was entranced by the stone and could not stop herself from moving it in the light to see the different colours reflected.

"Look into the ring, Rose and tell me what you see," ordered Luthian.

Rose gazed into the ring and felt its old magic begin working at once. It took her into another time and place where she could see the beginnings of all dragons and their powers. She saw the first dragon hatch and felt the wonder and joy of its being.

She saw the destruction of dragons by the Drogonians and she saw the turning of Apophis, a mighty dragon who had been converted by them to do their bidding and to help them in their quest to rule all lands.

"Do you understand?" asked Luthian gently lifting Rose's chin so that she would meet his gaze.

"Yes," said an awed Rose, "I do understand, I understand completely."

"It is now time to show you how to use the hour glass," said King Luthian, "as you have already seen many years ago dragons had the ability to teleport between places and time. This gift was taken away from them when they used it to destroy each other. The gift of teleporting was then placed into this hourglass to be used by the red dragon when her time came. The hour glass will be placed inside your dragon form and all you need to do if you want to activate it is to reach inside of yourself and turn it."

"But how do I take on my dragon form?"

" By holding your breath for a few minutes, until you find it very difficult to breathe and then without letting your breath out, take another deep breath," said Luthian, "quite simple if you concentrate very hard."

Rose struggled at first, but eventually managed the change. She changed backwards and forwards a few times just for good measure and then King Luthian lifted her breastplate upwards while she was in dragon form so that he could insert the hourglass.

"You are now ready," he said smiling.

# CHAPTER FOUR

## The Gathering

Time had seemed to stand still in the Freeland Citadel while the dragon apprentices were learning how to use their skills, but now it was almost daybreak and King Luthian invited both Rose and Vicky to witness the beginnings of a new day.

Dawn was a very special time at the citadel as it chased away the night with its dark shadows and woke the sun up. By the time the trio got to the courtyard in which the sun had spent the night, it was full of curious spectators who had arrived from near and far to watch the sun rise and to see the strangers!

King Luthian Summoner of Light, strode towards the great tripod with both his arms outstretched and then began to chant the ancient verse to wake the sun from its slumber.

*Sun behold*
*I bring you from the threshold*
*Listen now and hear my cry*
*Awaken to take your place in the sky.*

As the last verse of the magical rhyme was spoken, the sun appeared to tilt ever so slightly and then it began to move upwards. Vicky thought about a helium balloon she once had and how when the string broke it slowly floated just beyond her grasp and then higher and higher still until she could no longer reach it! The suns ascent reminded her of this moment!

" Come there is little time to waste," whispered the wind. Both Rose and Vicky appeared to have heard the whispering at the same time as they both turned in the direction that they had heard it coming from. " Good the time of the War Lords has begun! Look to the Protector of Truth and Keeper of Secrets they will lead the way that you must now follow with haste. I wish you God speed in your quest!" announced the King and then strode towards the Grand Hall they had eaten in the day before without a backward glance.

" This way if you please," announced both Salome and Fidel simultaneously. Mother and daughter found themselves following what appeared to be an ancient pathway that led to a huge flat outcrop that dominated its surroundings. Upon this outcrop stood Valour and others similarly dressed. Each person had a mount standing next to him or her. Rose's heart leapt with joy as she recognised Firefox.

"All hail the red dragon and time lord. All hail the crystal dragon whose breath bears wings! May they both live long and fight hard to return the peace that was promised to us by the ancients.

Rose felt very strange and a bit embarrassed to be greeted in this manner but decided that she could get used to it. She gazed at all those present and was delighted to see that Bling was part of the warring party. It was he who appeared to have Firefox as his mount.

"Muuuum, I think we are a couple of mounts short," stammered a disappointed Vicky. She did not want another ride similar to the one that they had arrived at the citadel on. She did not want to share a mount as she had found it very squashed and cramped!

"Ho ho, don't you know you will be flying to the Drogonian's fortress on your own steam."

"Our own steam? Whatever do you mean Bling?" asked a confused Rose.

"Enough of this idle chatter! There will be plenty of time for chit-chat when the war is over," exclaimed Salome. "Valour still needs to instruct you in the use of our weaponry and time is wasting!"

Valour had brought swords, a slingshot and armour for the two nymphs.

"Come with me Rose, so that we may begin your training. Vicky will accompany Stangor who will teach her how to be a masterful combater in the use of the slingshot and I will teach you the art of good swordsmanship!"

And so the training began!

"Relax! It is perfectly understandable to tense up in combat, but you must make every effort to stay calm," explained Valour. "Keep your body balanced so you can strike or parry without being hit! Watch your opponent's movements and learn when he moves in to attack so that you are able to launch a pre-emptive strike BUT you must be quick! Assess the situation.......everyone has a weakness; use this weakness against your opponent, but engage with care! If you charge in recklessly, especially against a trained fighter, he may just wait and let you impale yourself on his sword! By engaging carefully you will be able to maintain control and focus at all times.

Keep your elbows bent, and close to your body like this. Extend your sword towards your opponent, not your arms. Remember to remain calm and confident. If you are nervous or frightened, your opponent may try to take advantage of your lack of confidence!

The training was long and arduous and Rose felt that perhaps King Luthian had been too ambitious with the bestowing of the powers and the giving of his trust! After all Rose had been a housewife for a number of years, what did she know about sword fighting and war tactics?

"I think you are ready now," said the beautiful Valour, smiling for the first time. "You have done well and will be able to defend yourself in battle using your own prowess and the magic of the sword."

Stangor and Vicky were waiting on the outcrop with the rest of the assembled company by the time Valour and Rose arrived. Rose had a funny feeling that they had been there for quite some time because a closeness seemed to have developed amongst the gathered warriors and Vicky. Just for what was really a tiny second, she almost felt jealous of her daughter and then as quick as a wink she herself was been introduced to the noble warriors and their steeds. The group were now becoming restless and they were impatient to leave the outcrop. Rose felt a twinge of guilt for having kept them waiting for as long as she had, but knew that if she had not got the proper sword training and fighting techniques from Valour, she could not be counted on in battle

# The Warriors Take Flight

Both Rose and Vicky had realised during their combat training that they would be travelling in their dragon forms and this is why there had been no mounts ready and waiting for them!

"I must hold my breath and then hold it again," whispered Rose and Vicky simultaneously.

Both nymphs magically disappeared and dragons now stood where once they had been.

It had been many decades since the remaining and surviving dragons of Free Land had gathered together to restore the balance of law and order.

Warriors, mounts and Free Landers looked up in awe and amazement to see the red dragon, the crystal dragon and Fidel the Defender of Truth standing together at the gathering stone. "Come, we must be away," cried a triumphant Fidel, " Follow me."

All the warriors (who had been patiently waiting for this exact moment to begin) sprung onto their flying mounts, each one more beautiful than the next, but non more beautiful then the handsome Firefox who leapt up into the air so suddenly Bling almost fell off.

"I wish you had told me you were going to jump up like you did before you did it," grumbled Bling who now decided it was safer holding on to the horse with all four of his 'sticky' pads.

Vicky had never felt more alive in her entire life! She sensed the wind underneath her outstretched wings and enjoyed the enormous feeling of freedom her new found gift of flying had given her. She looked over to her left and saw the red dragon experiencing the same joy. To her right she spied Fidel with Salome astride his back perfectly balanced like an acrobat walking the high wire.

Below them, not too far away she could see Stangor on his flying mare. She felt a sudden rush of excitement and could not wait to reach their destination.

When Rose was younger she had had flying dreams, but she had never dreamed that flying would be so exhilarating! She felt the huge expanse of her dragon wings beating the air around her in order to gain height and speed. She was travelling too fast to take note of her surroundings, but did manage to catch Vicky's eye at one point and gave her a big wink!

Fidel led the party of warriors deeper and deeper into Drogonian claimed territory. He knew the land layout well as this was where he had been hatched as a nestling and discovered by a 'scouting' Freelander. For this he was glad, as he was sure if a Drogonian had discovered him in his formative years; his life would have been most unpleasant and very different. He would never have been given the title of Defender of Truth and he would never have met Salome his best friend and keeper.

Valour sat astride a flying unicorn, whose name had never been revealed to any Freelander. Both rider and mount were exquisitely beautiful. Valour had been raised as a defender and knew that one day her time would come to defend the ideals of all Freelanders. Her bosom welled up with pride for she knew that moment in time for which she had been born had finally arrived. The day of reckoning was fast approaching and she was one of the chosen War Lords. She had arranged to meet the horse people and the others two leagues South of the impenetrable fortress where a secret camp had already been set up and awaiting the arrival of her party.

# Luthian's Army

As soon as they landed Rose transformed herself back into nymph form. She looked around the camp. " Well, what do you think of King Luthian's army," asked Bling who had hastily dismounted as soon as Firefox's hooves had touched terra firma.

"Oh Bling it is everything I've ever dreamed or imagined possible and more but ….", It was at this point that Rose's huge big saucer like eyes filled with tears; she began to feel a deep sense of longing for her home and Frank. There was a feint smell of something vaguely familiar coming from the direction of the gossamer tents and it was this smell that had made her feel quite suddenly homesick.

"What is that smell Bling? I'm sure I've smelt it before, but can't quite put my finger on it?" At this point both Bling and Rose put their noses in the air and began to sniff.

"Why don't you go and investigate?" asked Bling trying very hard to hide the smile on his frog like face. "I'm sure it will all come back to you when you find out what is causing the aroma!"

Rose was rather puzzled by Blings sudden change in temperament as he had been grumpy for most of the flight, but was too polite to ask why he had spontaneously cheered up. She had no immediate plans so she decided that she would take Bling's advice and investigate the source of the aroma.

The pathway that she chose was rather narrow and seemed to meander aimlessly through the camp. A low fog had magically settled on the encampment to keep it hidden from the flying scouts of the Drogonians, who were constantly reporting back to their master of any strange or new goings on.

Visibility was poor, but Rose's sense of smell had become heightened since the bestowing of the powers by King Luthian. She followed her nose for what seemed a long time but in reality it had only been a couple of minutes, until she got to the edge of the encampment. She stopped and found herself to be in front of a huge tent. The tent was pale silver in colour with King Luthian's Coat of Arms sewn directly above the entrance in gold skein. Rose gasped as she stood outside the commander in chief's head quarters for just outside and to the left of the entrance was a little billycan warming over a small fire. It was from this billycan that the aroma she had been following was emanating! It was..., it was........,

"Frank!" Rose could not believe her eyes or her good fortune. Striding out of the tent was Frank who had come to check whether the billycan had boiled.

Frank looked up and saw Rose.

"Just in time for tea," he said smiling.
"But how......., how......? Rose finally understood the source of that vaguely familiar aroma. It had been herbal tea! Frank's herbal tea!

# Frank's Tale

No sooner had Rose and Vicky left 26 Elm Park Close when Frank's adventure had begun!

Left alone in the dimly lit kitchen and worried about his family he had decided to brew a pot of tea for himself. It was precisely at this moment when Stangor the True had arrived to rescue Bling.

"Who are you?" asked the disgruntled and lonely Frank, "and what is it you want?"

"I am Stangor the True. I have come to rescue Bling from all things vile and villainous."

"You are to late," sighed Frank, " he left 'bout half an hour ago with Rose and Vicky." Frank hoped this was true as he had no idea what had happened to Vicky. She had never returned after running out in the middle of the night.

"What is that strange but compelling aroma?" queried Stangor, sniffing the cup that was now in Frank's hands ready for consumption.

"Tea. Would you care for a cup before you leave?" Frank was always polite and never rude to a stranger even if they appeared in the middle of the night uninvited in his kitchen.

Stangor and Frank spent what seemed an hour or so sharing the pot of tea he had made. They were both quite comfortable and sleepy when Lillie arrived.

Lillie was a flying Unicorn. She had always kept her name a secret from Freelanders and Drogonians alike. She was a magical creature, who would fall under the command of any being that knew how to address her by using her name. Time was of the essence and she was in a hurry but she knew that if she were to enlist Frank's help she would need to introduce herself properly.

"My name is Lillie and I have been asked to whisk you to the encampment in Drogonia by King Luthian who has heard of your naval battle experiences and rope tying expertise. He would like you to help take command of his troops in the fight for Freelanders. Will you come?"

Frank was overwhelmed by all that had happened to him in one night but was eager to see his family again, so he did not hesitate in accepting the Unicorns offer.

"Great, I'll quickly get some clothes packed, and change into something more suitable and......"

"We leave immediately! There is no need or time to change!" Whinnied the beautiful creature. " You will have all that you require at the camp except for you home brew, you may bring some with you if you like," she offered.

Frank hastily packed a couple of bags of herbal tea and presented himself to Lillie for transportation. He noticed that Stangor was no longer in the room and wondered how he could have disappeared as quickly as he had done!

As I've already explained; Lillie is a magical creature; she slowly blew through her nostrils and sparkling pink dust started to fill the air. Frank watched in awe as the pink dust started to envelope him. He hoped he would not choke! He closed his eyes and held his breath for a tiny moment.

Slowly, ever so slowly Frank's curiosity got the better of him. He opened one eye, then another and then stared in amazement as he realised he was no longer in the comfort of his own home but in what appeared to be a desolate field with hundreds of gossamer tents lining the walkways!

"Greetings Commander, we have been awaiting your arrival," boomed the hundred or so Freelanders, half-casts and nymphs who stood to attention and waited for their new commander to speak.

Frank felt shy and awkward as he was still dressed in his pyjamas and had arrived on a pink cloud! Not something he would have chosen to do, but it did not seem to matter to the group of curious but well disciplined onlookers.

"Er…thank you for this fine assembly," replied Frank, " is there somewhere I can change?"

He was led to a very large and beautiful pale silver tent that had King Luthian's Family Crest embroidered over the entrance in gold skein.

Inside the tent were all the things he would need for his personal care as well as some proposed battle plans for the impending skirmish. Laying next to the plans was a huge golden envelope addressed to him. Frank opened the envelope and felt the magic escape from its encasement and enter the addressee. This was Frank's bestowing of powers.

He could feel a new strength coursing through his veins and an understanding of everything that had been before and was about to become! He had power and knowledge beyond his wildest dreams and a strong determined sense of loyalty for the king he was yet to meet.

Looking down he suddenly understood Lillie's reasons for stating he would not need to pack any clothing; for he was no longer man, but a combination of man and four legged beast! He was a centaur! A dashing, magnificent centaur!

"Commander," whinnied a familiar voice outside the tent, "we would like to know if you are ready to discuss the battle plans and fighting strategies?"

It was Lillie, who had just arrived and was pleased to see that Frank had settled in and had opened his envelope.

"Yes, please come inside and let the preparations begin!"

It had been Frank's idea to cloak the camp in a magical fog to keep it safe from the eyes of the enemy and it had been Lillie who had made it happen.
"But," admonished Frank, " make sure that it is not pink!"

Lillie laughed (a special tinkling sound that spreads happiness whenever and wherever it is heard).

"Don't worry," she giggled "pink is only used for transporting."

After the magic had been done, Lillie took her leave of Frank with a promise that he would never reveal her name to any Freelander or Drogonian even under the pain of death!

"I'm curious why did you reveal it to me?"

"I was been polite and needed you to listen to me! Besides you are neither Freelander or Drogonian," she whinnied and rose into the air with the grace and ease that only magical unicorns have.

# CHAPTER 5

## Settling In

Vicky was feeling both nervous and excited as she landed in the open field that was now the army's encampment. She saw her mother chatting to Bling and then disappear into the mist. She wondered where Rose was going and was about to follow her when Stangor the True, her fighting mentor appeared at her side.

"Would you like me to show you around the encampment," he asked politely. " I can introduce you to some of the others, but you will have to change back into your nymph form," he admonished; smiling at her forgetfulness and thinking about what it was like to be young again.

It was only then that Vicky realised that she was still in her Dragon form and had carelessly stood on a couple of tent ropes!

"Oops, how absentminded of me," she gasped, and changed back into her nymph form. "I hope I haven't caused too much damage!"

Stangor took Vicky into the middle of the camp and introduced her to several of the King's loyal subjects.

Valour sentinel of the citadel watched longingly from a distance and felt a new and strange unpleasant sensation deep within her chest. She and Stangor had been friends for the longest of times and she had wanted to spend the eve of battlement alone with him. She soon realised that this was impossible and decided to join both Stangor and Vicky.

Vicky felt honoured and pleased that Stangor and Valour would both choose to spend time with her. She was so refreshingly innocent that in no time at all Valour lost her feelings of jealousy and was glad that she had chosen to join them!

Bling heard sounds of merriment and decided to join the merry-makers. To his astonishment and delight he saw Vicky sitting amongst Luthian's warriors enjoying a light meal of special goat's milk broth and a bottle of wine.

"Oh my, oh my, how time does fly," said Bling as he sat down. "Just a short time ago you were drinking tea in the kitchen and now you are drinking wine before a great battle!"

"What!......Oh it's you Bling......where is Rose?.... have you seen her?", asked Vicky.

"She's down in the valley with the commander drinking herbal tea," replied Bling.

"Why on earth is she with the commander and where in the world did she get more tea?" asked a surprised Vicky for she was sure that they had finished the last of the sticky, sweet herbal beverage whilst travelling to the citadel.

" The commander is Frank", said Bling matter of fact, as though he had been expecting her to know!

"What!….Frank….. here?.….Why didn't anyone tell me? Bling, darling Bling, please, oh please take me to see the commander straight away!" cried an excited Vicky.

"Mmmmph…….. now suddenly it's my darling is it! Only when you want something from me or expect me to do something for you, is when I'm your darling!"

"Oh dear Bling, that's certainly not true! I could have asked anybody here to escort me to the commander's tent as I'm sure everybody but me knows where it is!" replied an exasperated Vicky.

It took Bling a moment to think about this and then he realised that this was true. He apologised for been such a grump and took Vicky by the hand to escort her to the commander's tent.

# Reunited

Walking beside Bling and following the well-worn path, Vicky noticed that all the inhabitants of the camp were getting ready for the impending battle. She suddenly became overwhelmed with the magnitude of what she and her mother had promised King Luthian and was starting to feel just a little afraid when the same familiar smell that had first brought Rose to the commander-in-chiefs tent began to tickle her olfactory senses.

'Mmmm, I remember that smell ..... it's ever so familiar and .........deliciously aromatic and ...............
Frank!' Vicky ran into the arms of her father and began to sob uncontrollably.
'I missed you and I missed your tea,' she hiccupped trying to control the urge to cry.

'Remember when you were a little girl and I would rock you on my knee and tell you everything would turn out just fine?' smiled Frank, 'well...er, this is one of those times except you're not little any more and I don't have a knee to rock you with!' guffawed Frank.

Vicky started to laugh and her tears of sadness changed into tears of joy! 'Can I have a mug of your delicious tea,' she asked smiling.

Rose and Vicky had always taken the mick out of Frank because of his fondness of making herbal tea in times of trouble, but now that very same act felt comforting and it filled them with a sense of well being the likes of which they had not felt since arriving in this strange magical land.

Late into the night Frank and his family sat in front of his campfire telling and sometimes retelling each other about the adventures that they had had since leaving their home.

They sat in front of the dying coal embers reminiscing with fondness the kinds of things that normal families do when they have not been called into a strange land to fight in a battle.

At this point Bling had cautiously crept away from the family and decided to join Stangor's
party who he hoped were still busy eating broth and drinking wine. Looking back towards the commander-in-chief's tent he had an overwhelming sense of loneliness and suddenly felt in great need of company.

'Bling? Bling? Is that really you?' asked a small frog like creature standing at the entrance to one of the gossamer tents lower in the valley.

Bling turned in the direction of the voice and stood still for a moment rubbing his eyes. 'Blog, Blog is that you?' he cried in an instant of recognition.

Both strange frog like creatures hopped in a most hurriedly fashion and threw their arms around each other. "Oh Blog it has been years since I last saw you," exclaimed

Bling. "I thought you had been killed or worse still you had been forced to work in the leaf fields by the Drogonians!"

Blog was Blings younger sibling by two decades and Bling had always watched out for him until one day he had returned to Moth Hall to find that his family had disappeared and a Drogonian had moved into their ancestral home. He had always felt guilty because he was not there to save his family.

The two brothers hugged each other for what seemed an eternity and then sat down next to Blog's campfire reminiscing about the good and bad times they'd had together and then telling each other what had become of them and what they had done since leaving Moth Hall.

'Oh Bling, you are a true hero,' sighed Blog dreamily ' I hope that I can be as brave as you tomorrow. Why, if it had not been for you we would not have had the red and crystal dragons nor would we have had such a fine commander-in-chief!'

Bling blinked twice in the firelight and thought about what Blog had said. He had never thought of himself a hero, nor had anyone ever called him that. He was glad to have met up with Blog again and all the guilt that he had ever carried around with him suddenly disappeared with the utterance of these words: - 'you are a true hero.'

# Breaking Camp

Night seemed to have passed quickly in the camp of the warlords. As day dawned there was an eerie hush that seemed to fall on the camp as all the combatants prepared to break camp.

Tents were broken down, bedding was rolled and utensils were all packed away into the light weight bags each soldier carried with him.

The mist that Lillie had magically conjured up to surround the encampment became more oppressive and visibility was very poor. Frank did not want to take any chances of the Drogonian spies seeing all the commotion and warning their enemies of their imminent arrival.

Rose was surprised and concerned that Frank had not shared any of his battle plans with her or Vicky and was secretly very worried about this. Last night was fun but morning had crept up too suddenly and not allowed them time to discuss the impending battle.

'What are we going to do?' whispered Vicky sensing her mother's unease. Like a well-drilled army the rest of the camp seemed to know what was expected of them and got on with it with no fuss or trouble.

'I'm not sure, Vicky dear, but I am sure we will find out in good time. At least that is what I hope!' stated Rose a little too nervously to convince Vicky that she was not worried.

'Right whose for a mug of hot herbal tea then?' Franks cheerful voice boomed through the opening of the tent where Rose and Vicky had spent the night.

'Oh Frank how could you think of making us tea on such a day as this?' sobbed Rose.

'Drink first and then we will discuss how you are feeling,' suggested Frank smiling.

Both Vicky and Rose obediently took the mugs proffered them and silently contemplated the day ahead of them. What would the outcome of this battle be? Would they ever return to 26 Elm Park Close? But most of all would life ever be normal again!

Drinking slowly and pondering on all these questions, a most magical thing began to happen to both nymphs! They suddenly became aware of all their duties and what function that they would serve in the up and coming battle. If Frank's plan worked there might not even be a battle!

Frank's tea was magical! It filled you with warmth and knowledge and allowed you to become one with all who drank from it. Luthian's army had gained a shared knowledge and shared consciousness through Frank's magical tea leaves! No words needed to be spoken; for thoughts were conveyed from one to another in a blink of an eye! No wonder everyone had praised Frank during last nights festivities, for all of them had drank the magical formula, that is, all of them except Rose and Violet until now!

Reassured and confident in the knowledge of what to do raised Rose and Vicky's spirits so much that they gladly assisted Frank in breaking down his tent and packing away all the other stuff!

When all was done and ready the 'to arms' cry was sounded. In unison the mixed match of humans, dragons, nymphs, centaurs, changelings and others to numerous to mention stood to attention and shouted in one voice 'for Luthian and the Freeland!'

## Army On The Move

Both Rose and Vicky held their breath for what seemed to them ages and ever so slowly the nymphs began to disappear and in their place stood two dragons. Frank had never seen his wife and daughter in their dragon form and stood and marvelled at this wondrous sight!

'Vicky it's time', whispered a soft voice just behind her ear. As if by magic, which of course it was, Vicky began to blow crystal bubbles to help transport the foot soldiers invisibly.

Almost instantaneously and at the same time, Rose lifted her dragon breastplate, reached inside of herself and turned the hourglass.

At first Frank thought the mist had become thicker than pea soup because he could not see the Red Dragon or Bling. They both seemed to have disappeared in what appeared to be a millisecond. He stood still and rubbed his eyes.

'She's gone,' said Vicky matter of fact. 'The hourglass allows her to teleport herself and anyone touching her to any destination in the world...... or rather, what I mean is....Freeland,' which of course was not necessary as Frank already knew the answer because he could read Vicky's thoughts now that she had drank the magical tea leaves!!

Soon the air was filled with crystal bubbles big enough for a man, centaur or dwarf to get into. In a very orderly fashion each foot soldier climbed into their crystal ball and patiently waited for the wind to lift them to the Drogonian fortress.

Vicky was beginning to feel quiet dizzy from blowing bubbles when she spotted a familiar face trying to get into his crystal carriage but not quite getting it right as the bubble had lifted too far off the ground. 'I never thought that I would see you again my dear friend and tutor!' She cried jubilantly.

'Mmmmrph,' answered Magpop who was still as short tempered as ever. 'You need to blow these crazy balls closer to the ground for the likes of me self!'
Vicky was delighted to have spotted Magpop, for he alone knew what her full capabilities were and how she could summon her magical powers for he had been her

tutor in the magical arts when she had received her gifts and powers from King Luthian.

'Will you travel with me and be my guide,' asked Vicky who felt that she needed company and who better than Magpop! This offer delighted Magpop who liked to look important and feel special. Being a dwarf is not easy because most people tend to over look you or sometimes they even look straight past you! This was just the type of offer Magpop needed and he accepted with a great deal of huffing and puffing and self-importance.

# CHAPTER 6

## Apophis' Lair

Rose found herself inside a cold, wet and gloomy looking cave. Behind her she could see the entrance to the cave but the light outside appeared to be just as cold, wet and gloomy as the cave itself! She turned her head slowly and noticed a quick movement in the periphery of her vision. Squinting in the darkness she could just make out a tiny frog-like shape.

'Bling is that you?' she whispered, using her dragon's breathe to direct her faint voice to the creature. The creature appeared to wobble in front of her and then bounded in one huge big agile leap to her side.

'We have lots of work to do before Luthian's men get here,' said Bling; ' and you need to follow my instructions very carefully otherwise we may fail in our endeavours to stop a full scale battle taking place.

'Oh,' smiled a pleasantly surprised Rose, ' I am glad you are here as I thought that I would be on my own!' Rose did not want to admit that she was a tiny bit frightened even in her dragon form and she felt a huge sense of relief washing over all her anxieties knowing that Bling would share this new adventure with her.

'Where are we?' she whispered.

'We are in the heart of Drogonia, the resting place of Apophis, royal guardian, friend and pet of the Lord Drogonia.' stated Bling trying to sound confident, brave and hero like!

Rose knew who Apophis was for she had the power of the Dragon Stone to guide her in the knowledge of all dragons. Apophis, the dragon; had been reared by the Drogonians to do their bidding just as she in Red Dragon form was compelled to help King Luthian. Apophis was Roses nemesis!

'Oh my, what if he finds us in his lair?'

'He already knows that we are here,' stated a less then brave Bling, ' he can sense your presence through the Dragon Stone and is approaching us as I speak. Can you sense his imminent arrival Rose?'

Suddenly Rose understood the origin of this impending sense of doom. It was not how she was feeling but her sensing the approaching Apophis!

'Wh…..wh…. what are we going to do?' asked a nervous and anxious Rose.

'You are going to convince Apophis that you are his ally and not his enemy,' said Bling.

'But how am I going to do that Bling? He will know that I am his enemy as soon as he lays his eyes upon me!' groaned Rose who felt that the strain of loosing his home and family had eventually caught up with Bling and he was no longer thinking very clearly.

'You are going to use the power of the Dragon Stone to convince him that you are his friend and ally the Crimson Dragon.' stated Bling and then went on further to add who the Crimson Dragon was for our benefit as Rose already knew since she was wearing the Dragon Stone!

'The prophecy of the Crimson Dragon states that the Crimson Dragon will rise up from the murky and muddy waters of Apophis' lair to lure the enemies of Drogonia into a trap of great cunning and it is then that the Drogonian armies will defeat King Luthian's warlords and they that survive this slaughter shall be captured and henceforth serve King Drogonia!'

Rose gasped and then asked, 'but …..but what happens when the real Crimson Dragon arrives and finds me attempting to impersonate it?'

'You are the real Crimson Dragon Rose. It was King Luthian who planted this false prophecy into the book of prophets many decades ago. He knew that one day there would be a final battle for the control of Freeland and hoped that with this false prophecy he would be able to avoid any unnecessary blood shed for he is the Summoner of light and not a warlord!' stated Bling. ' Now,' he continued ' it is time to put our plan into action! You need to lie down on the floor of Apophis' lair whilst I summon the water to cover you and when you sense that Apophis is inside this part of the lair you are to rise slowly out of the mud and water!'

Rose followed Bling's instructions and slowly sank onto the muddy floor of the cavern. Bling, guardian of water, summoned the water sprites into Apophis' lair and instructed them to cover Rose from top to tail. In the blink of an eye and faster then you can say 'kalazam,' the sprites became thousands of droplets of water and rained over Rose, filling the cavern and covering Rose from head to tail!

Rose held her breath and waited for the moment that Apophis would arrive. During the time that she held her breathe and closed her eyes it felt like a hundred years had passed and she wondered if he would ever arrive and this elaborate plan and ruse had all been for nothing!

## The Crimson Dragon

Rose felt the exact moment Apophis entered this unused part of the cave. She sensed his awareness of her and even though she was under thousands of droplets of water she was sure that she could smell him! She began to rise out of the water slowly, ever so slowly, taking care not to tread on any of the water sprites that had come to her aid in this deception. Finally with one last burst of energy she emerged out of the depths of the muddy water …. Crimson! The effect of the mud on her red dragon scales was quite startling. It had changed her colour from shades of red to a dull, indistinguishable shade of crimson. Rose was now the Crimson Dragon!

At last the prophecy was coming into being; or at least that is what it appeared like to Apophis. Rose stared at the almost pitch black dragon in front of her and for one tiny miniscule second she felt sorry for him, but then remembered his part in the destruction of Freeland and could not help herself from feeling anger and hatred towards the huge beast and its captors, who now stood before her in amazement and wonderment.

'Is it time?' asked the startled black dragon trying to recover some of his composure and fierceness!

'Not quite yet,' answered Rose, 'we need to time our plan to perfection otherwise it will not work. Take me to your king,' she demanded.

Apophis reeled around in the tight space of the entrance to the cavern and asked Rose to follow him. Gingerly she waded through the mud and made her way up the embankment to what she hoped would be the Freelanders inevitable freedom.

Once outside the entrance to the cave Rose surveyed her surroundings. She could not help but admire Apophis for his choice of abode, for from the ridge that they now stood upon she could not only see the entire fortress and it's inhabitants but the surrounding area for miles on either side! King Luthian's army would be easily spotted if they marched on to the fortress. She was glad that Vicky had followed her into this adventure, as the Freelanders definitely needed the power of the Crystal Dragon!

Now that she stood outside the entrance to the dragon's lair she would need to summon the wind to bring the floating balls that were filled with Luthian's troops and direct the assault team into the fortress so that an alarm could not be raised, and no one would be aware of their presence until it was to late!

Knowing that it would not be an easy task to accomplish standing next to Apophis, she decided to try and direct his attention elsewhere while she summoned the winds.

'You have a very strong position from your lair. You were very wise and clever to make this your abode.' She said, trying to flatter the huge beast, remembering a fable that her mother once told her about flattery. She hoped that her trick would work as well as it had done in the fable!

Apophis regarded her silently and began to smile. It was a very scary smile showing all his dragon teeth, but at least he was off guard for the moment. Then something wonderful happened. Apophis took the bait and began to boast about how he had added extra space and peep holes throughout the lair.

While he was expounding his contribution to the numerous caverns, Rose took the opportunity to summon the four winds!  She summoned the North wind first, followed by the South and then the East and West winds. She found it difficult to summon the winds without raising Apophis' suspicions but her plan worked well and he seemed to be none the wiser!

'North wind, North wind come now to my aid,
pursue my breath before it begins to fade;
Lift the baubles of the crystal dragon's snort,
and bring them here to Drogonia's fort.


South wind, South wind hear my plea,
I need your help to set the Freelanders free;
Bring the baubles that I seek,
and place them at King Drogonia's feet.

East and West,
your help is needed in this quest;
Please aid the South and North,
and together bring the soldiers forth.

Rose completed her spell in the nick of time!  Apophis had just finished his tirade and was eager to seek audience with king Drogonia and to introduce the king to the Crimson Dragon who it was foretold would save the leaf eating colonies! He was glad he had been in his lair at the time of her arrival as now he could claim great rewards from the king and soon, yes oh very soon dispose of him altogether! For the Black Dragon had plans of his very own and these did not include the Drogonian king who had enslaved him for many years.

The two huge beasts lifted their wings and soared into the air as graceful as a pair of swans! They circled the fortress three times before alighting in the courtyard because Apophis wanted to make sure that everyone in Drogonia had witnessed his arrival with the Crimson Dragon! He was sure that she would follow him in this display of vanity and was rather pleased when she did!

The landing was not as graceful as the taking off and Rose found it hard not to misjudge and land outside the courtyard walls. She had to concentrate very hard and managed to manoeuvre her big body downward just in time to land within inches of the courtyard walls.

There was a flurry of excitement and then a hush as both Apophis and the Crimson Dragon skidded to a halt barely missing the courtiers who had gathered in the courtyard to witness their arrival.

# Bling's Mission

Bling had undertaken to scout around the various buildings within the fortress walls itself. He had the ability to make himself invisible and therefore had volunteered his services for this dangerous mission. He did not disclose this information to Rose, as he knew she would be concerned for his safety and as a result may impede her own!

Whilst Rose busied herself in distracting Apophis and summoning the four winds, Bling had become invisible and had noiselessly and furtively climbed down the edge of the mountainous cliff, using his sticky pads to cling to the smooth surface of the treacherous slope. It seemed to take an age before he managed to climb down to the bottom of the valley where the fortress walls loomed ominously in front of him.

Cautiously and quietly Bling scaled the walls of the fortress. He found himself standing in what appeared to be an arena of sorts. It reminded him of a bull fighting ring and he shivered at the thought of what may lie beyond within the confines of the well guarded and locked gates that opened into the arena!

He was still contemplating how to gain entry into the well-guarded space when he noticed a turtle like creature moving towards the gates. On the creatures back was a tablecloth and what appeared to be a very frugal meal! Bling found himself wondering for whom this meagre meal was for when he felt himself compelled to follow it and hurried to close the distance between the two of them. As the turtle and Bling neared the gates; the gates began to creak and unlock by their own accord as if by magic which as you and I know it most certainly was! Bling could not believe his luck; it had been extremely lucky to arrive in the arena at the same time as this creature!

Bling found himself in a maze of tunnels, each one headed off in a different direction. He was glad that he did not have to circumnavigate these corridors on his own!

'Well aren't you going to introduce yourself?' snapped the turtle to his invisible companion.

Bling felt most uncomfortable when he realised that the turtle knew of his presence and hurriedly turned himself visible once more.

'Er…Bling at your service sir and who might you be?' he replied most politely, for this strange creature had been aware of him the whole time and had not alerted the guards to his being there!

'Trinidad …… the bearer of tidings.' answered the turtle in a most polite way.
' Now that the formalities are over; why did you follow me into the forbidden zone?' he questioned.

Bling found that he could not lie to this strange but friendly creature; he felt compelled to tell it the truth about his mission, as much as he had felt compelled to follow it. 'I….I ….have been sent by King Luthian's guard to scout the fortress and what lies within it's walls.' he stammered.

# The Forbidden Zone

'What is the forbidden zone?' asked Bling whose curiosity had been aroused by the complete lack of reaction from Trinidad when he had announced his true purpose for being inside the fortress; a spy sent by the Freelanders.

'The forbidden zone is where all the enemies of the Drogonian's are kept', replied Trinidad.

Bling gasped and found himself turning a purple - blue colour; for he could not turn white when he was frightened. ' Er ... is that why I felt compelled to follow you into the forbidden zone,' groaned Bling. 'Am I now a prisoner?'

'Good heavens no,' laughed Trinidad 'I think Kyron made you follow me so that you can assist in his escape.'

'Who on Freeland is Kyron?'

' He is He who created the colonies and those that live within it's walls.' replied Trinidad.

'King Luthian's brother?' asked a startled Bling. He could not believe that he had had the misfortune of falling into this trap sprung by the Drogonian Lord! He felt annoyed with himself for following Trinidad into the forbidden zone and wondered if his friends would ever find him or if he would ever walk out of this dark prison alive!

"Oh , no.........what would Kyron want to see me for? I am sure he's made a mistake calling me here! Please could you escort me back to the gates and then I'll figure out a way to get out of the arena without been seen if you don't mind."

Bling tried to pressure Trinidad into letting him go but the turtle could not be swayed. He was determined to deliver the meal and Bling along with the meal!

He knew, that all good colonists were rewarded and he was looking forward to an early retirement!

Bling reluctantly followed Trinidad feeling betrayed and useless. He no longer felt like a true hero and wondered if he would ever see his beloved brother Blog again!

A door at the far end of the passage slowly unlocked itself for Trinidad and Bling to gain access into the room that lay beyond.

It took a while for Bling's vision to adjust to the light in this room, as he had been walking in darkened passageways for what seemed an eternity. He wished that he were still in the labyrinth of passages with poor visibility rather then entering this slightly illuminated room!

# CHAPTER 7

## A Surprise Ally

Bling surveyed the room that he was now standing in with both curiosity and dread. In the far corner of the dimly lit room he noticed a bed with a table standing next to it. On the table was the light which offered the room its only illumination. In the opposite corner was an old chair that had seen better days and had very little stuffing left. The springs were beginning to tear through the once velveteen fabric and one of the arm rests was missing! In front of this sad looking armchair stood a tall grey haired man!

Bling was surprised to see how similar this man was in looks to his brother King Luthian; but then on reflection he soon realised that it should not have been much of a surprise as both King Luthian and this man were twins!

"Please come in and sit down both of you."

Trinidad made his way to his usual spot in front of the armchair and slowly sank to the ground, by withdrawing his ancient limbs into his shell that doubled as a serving table. Poor Bling was uncertain as to where he should sit because there was only one chair and by Trinidad's actions he guessed that this is where Kyron would be sitting to have his meal.

"Please, make yourself comfortable on the floor next to Trinidad."

Rather cautiously Bling made his way to the spot that Kyron was indicating and sat down on the hard stone floor; blinking in the half light and wishing that he could be elsewhere.

When both creatures looked as though they were comfortable, Kyron sat down in the ancient armchair which seemed to groan under his weight! This surprised Bling as Kyron was not a very large man, due to the fact that he had been held captive for a long time and had to exist on the small scraps of food Trinidad brought to him once a day.

Seated now, Kyron picked up the threadbare linen napkin and unfolded it with a flourish! He then lifted the domed lid that had been placed over the porcelain dish in order to keep the flies from settling on it. In the middle of the plate was one single piece of bread and a mug of water! Kyron lifted the bread to his mouth and took a small bite. He chewed on this for ages, or so it seemed, relishing the flavour and the texture. He then picked up his mug of water, took a sip and swilled it round his mouth as though it were a fine wine, and finally swallowing it, with the few remaining bits of bread that had stuck between his teeth.

Bling watched in fascination. He had never in his life seen so much care taken while eating! This is what King's must look like when they eat he decided, as he has never seen a king eating before!

No words were spoken during the entire meal. Finally Kyron finished the last of his bread and water, wiped his mouth ever so carefully and placed the napkin back on Trinidad's shell.

"Thank you Trinidad, as always you have been an excellent dinner companion. I will miss your company until next time."

With these words the turtle got up slowly and made his way to the door. Once again the door opened in order for him to leave and then shut.

Trinidad knew that there was something important for him to do, but he could not remember what it was! He tried desperately to search his memory and to replay what had happened to him this day, but try as he might he could not remember! Oh well he thought 'it must be my age making me forget.....I'm not as young as I used to be!'

Kyron had guessed correctly that Trinidad was about to betray him and report Blings whereabouts to the council so he had used one of his mind bending techniques to erase Bling from Trinidad's memory.

Bling, now desperate to find an escape route began searching from his view point when he realised that Kyron's gaze was now focused on him.

"Come closer Bling and let me have a look at you." Hesitantly Bling hopped nearer to Kyron and sat down once again.

"How much like your father you are."
"You know my father?"

"Yes, your father and I have known each other for a long time Bling. We are friends and I miss his company."

This comment surprised Bling and he wondered when his father and Kyron had become friends and where his father was now.

"Your father, your mother and your two sisters were captured many years ago by the Drogonian warlords who wanted to lay claim to your father's birthright.......Moth Hall."

"Where......where is my family now and what became of them?"

"Your father, mother and sisters are safe. They now work in the kitchens of the Dark Citadel preparing tasty dishes for the warlords. It was your mother who baked the bread that was brought to me for lunch. If it had not been for your family's kindness and knowledge of herbs I think I would have died a long time ago. For the bread that is carefully and lovingly baked and fed to me each day has all the vitamins and proteins in it that I need in order to survive. Your mother conceals all this goodness in that one slice of bread everyday.........so that the Drogonians are none the wiser and because of this they believe me to have super powers!"

Bling could not believe his good fortune! To know that his family were alive and well was a great relief to him, however, he was a bit concerned that they were been forced to work in the kitchens of this dismal place!

Smiling, Kyron continued his story; "It seems so many years ago that I last saw my family. How is Luthian? Is he still alive? Does he continue to raise the sun every morning and put it to bed at night?"

Bling was uncertain as to whether he should be giving Kyron this information, but then decided that Kyron had been kind enough to share news about his family and that the least he could do was answer the questions that he had asked.

"King Luthian is still very much alive and he still tends to the sun ceremonies every morning and every night."

"This is indeed good news Bling. I am glad that no disasters have befallen him as I would have been unable to forgive myself......for it is I that created the Drogonians and it is I who now suffer for this mistake that I made so long ago I can only vaguely remember my reasons for doing so!"

Bling was not sure what to make of this, so decided not to interrupt him by trying to make small talk. He decided it would be better to listen and not say a word, which for any of you who know him; must realise that this was a very hard thing for him to do!

# Kyron's Story

"It was many years ago that the story of the Drogonians began! Like my Brother Luthian, I too wanted to make our games more interesting!

The beginning of this terrible legacy began as innocently as that! Together we created the first simple creatures that were used in our games."

Bling was not sure how he felt about Freelanders referred to as a game and struggled not to say anything rude!

"As time passed and we were getting older we became bored of what then seemed a pointless game; so we decided it was time to put the game away! In order to do this we had agreed that we would give our creatures free will, but still maintain responsibility for them."

Bling was starting to feel a bit agitated as he knew this story of the beginning. In fact all Freelanders and Drogonians were told this story and 'The Beginning' as it was now called was celebrated every year with festivities and the giving of gifts! He almost felt compelled to tell Kyron to get to the point of his story, but then decided that this would not be a very good idea! What if Kyron got mad? What would happen to him then? Would he be turned to dust or stone? No, he decided it would be best if he continued to listen politely!

"Eventually all creatures had free will and did not depend on us their creators for advice or guidance. Believe it or not we were very pleased that our creations had become so self sufficient and did not realise that the games we had played as children would come back to haunt us! When the creatures were first created they had no idea of good or evil! They were all innocent, both Freelanders and Drogonians alike! Luthian always played fair, but unfortunately it was I that liked to win. I wanted to win so badly that I did not once stop to think about the consequences of my actions! It was me that introduced the Drogonians to their war strategies and desire to imprison and dominate those that they had captured!"

Although Bling knew that this happened; he was surprised that Kyron was so willing to take all the blame and even more surprisingly, Bling started to feel sorry for the man!

"Eventually all that was secret and forbidden became known to the Drogonians and mind control techniques

Although he was still invisible, Bling's arrival in the
[fore]st did not go unnoticed by the sentry who was on
[duty.]

"Halt! Who goes there?"

Making himself visible and facing the direction
[in] where he had heard the voice coming from, Bling
[intro]duced himself.

[S]tepping out from behind a huge oak tree where he
[had] concealed himself, the sentry smiled and welcomed
[him]. "Come, the commander has been expecting your
[arriv]al."

[F]eeling very important and proud of himself, Bling
[follo]wed the sentry who was making his way further into
[the fo]rest towards a small clearing surrounded by a ring of
[ancie]nt and gnarled oak trees who were in what appeared
[to be] a deep conversation with the commander and the
[Crys]tal Dragon.

# Reporting To The Commander

[B]ling carefully picked his way through the dense
[unde]rgrowth of the forest, following in the footsteps of
[the se]ntry who was trying hard not to walk too quickly in
[his ex]citement!

"[S]ir may I interrupt you to announce the arrival of
[...]"

were taught to all the officers in charge of the common
Drogonian soldiers. They used this knowledge to enslave
and entrap the innocent and now I believe they have taken
their skills above earth. Is this true?"

"Unfortunately yes; there has been some evidence of
this." answered Bling, hoping that Kyron would continue
his tale of how he had landed up as the Drogonian's
prisoner and no longer their master!

Kyron was quiet for some time, carefully considering
this information, before continuing his story.

"I was afraid that one day this would happen. My
only surprise is that it has happened so soon! I thought
it would be many more years before the Drogonians
discovered another world above ours! I am truly sorry
that this has happened and believe me if I could undo any
of it I certainly would!"

It was at this point in the tale that Bling noticed Kyron
staring at the wall opposite him. If Bling had possessed
hair at the back of his neck, it would have been at this
point that they would have stood up! Shifting his gaze
from Kyron to the wall directly behind him; Bling did not
know what to expect or what it was that he might see! All
he knew was that suddenly he felt very trapped and if he
could he would have fled from that room in that instance
never to return!

# Escape From Captivity!

Both Kyron and Bling were now staring at the wall which began to shimmer and slowly disappear! Bling felt his heart leap and jump wildly in fear and dread! The atmosphere in the room was now tense with dreaded expectation.

"You! What are you doing here?" roared the massive Drogonian standing in the space where once a wall had stood. "Why aren't you in the kitchens?"

Bling could not believe his luck! This fierce looking Drogonian had mistaken him for his father! "I, I ........"

"Leave us at once!"

Bling needed no further invitation to leave the room! He scuttled past the huge bear-like creature without a backward glance and found himself in a long corridor with heavy closed doors on either side; leading to two flights of stairs that branched off in two different directions. Confused and unsure which flight of stairs to take, he hesitated for a millisecond and then decided to try going down the flight of stairs on his left hand side. As he approached the staircase he noticed that it had a well polished and smooth banister. As quick as a wink he jumped astride the banister. Facing the corridor and using the wall to push against, he flew down the banister lickety, split!

Thud! Thump! Bump! Ouch! Bli
a heap on the floor of a huge, deserted a
hall. Picking himself up from the flo
bottom, he took stock of himself and h

The round entrance hall had one
from it and several smaller doors. In ac
there were several round windows
heights around the room! This architec
to be ideal for Bling to see where he wa
toes and steadying himself with his ha
reach and look through the lower winc
To his surprise and delight he was
Apophis and the 'Crimson' dragon lan
No wonder the corridors, stairwells
were so deserted! Everyone was ou
arrival of the 'Crimson' dragon and A
very fortunate for Bling as he could n
without anyone knowing or raising the

Turning himself invisible, Bling
main door hoping that he would be abl
too much difficulty. Much to his su
standing slightly ajar and he was able
been noticed!

Once inside the courtyard Bling
way to the drawbridge which had beer
lowered in the excitement! Thankful
Bling made his way quickly and quiet
and towards the surrounding forest w
army were waiting for word from the

Frank, the Crystal Dragon and the trees all stopped in mid-conversation, to welcome Bling back from his dangerous spying mission.

"Well Bling, you little rascal, you managed to get in and out of the Citadel without raising any alarms. Well done! I am really pleased with you!"

A hush now fell in the open glade as everyone waited expectantly for Bling to speak.

"Thank you sir, I am pleased to have been of service to you. I do have some very good but surprising news for the king"

"Anything you tell me will be available to the king immediately", assured Frank.

"Well sir, as I entered into the Citadel, I noticed a creature carrying food. I felt compelled to follow this creature that was making his way towards the dungeons of the citadel............"

Bling was thoroughly enjoying himself in the retelling of his heroic deeds, pausing every now and then for dramatic effect!

Soon Bling had attracted a huge audience and he was pleased to note that Blog was one of those who had come to listen to his great tale of escape!

As Bling's tale was coming to a close and he had reached the point in his story where he had been mistaken for his father, Blog squealed with delight! Like Bling he had been unaware of what had happened to his family and had assumed the worse, supposing all of them to have been captured and tortured to death! This indeed was good news and he could hardly wait to speak to Bling in private so they could celebrate this good news!

As the tale came to an end; Frank became deep in thought. Like Bling he was both surprised by the capture of Kyron but concerned whether Kyron could be trusted as an ally!

Bling took this moment of deep contemplation as a sign that his company was no longer required and both he and Blog slipped out of the clearing almost unnoticed!

# Chapter 8

## Army On The Move

On hearing that the drawbridge was unmanned and unguarded Frank took the decision to mobilise the armed forces immediately! An opportunity like this was not an opportunity to be missed; he had to act very quickly!

The call to arms was sounded and like a well oiled machine the soldiers filed into their ranks without a whisper; expectantly, waiting for their commander to give them their marching orders.

Flanked by the Crystal Dragon and Salome astride Fidel, Frank and Valour turned towards this brave and trusting army.

"Today we fight for truth and freedom! May the sun be behind you and the wind in front, let us catch this fish while the water is disturbed!"

This may seem like a strange thing to say to an army going into battle, but Frank knew if the enemy's attention was elsewhere they would not be expecting an attack! Further more he could see that the sun was in an advantageous position for the army as it would mean that the enemy would have to look into the sun in order to fight them; this would give the Freelanders another advantage! Every thing now depended on the ability of the Freelander army to secure the occupation of the citadel with as little bloodshed as possible! Once again they were to make use of the invisi-bubbles so that they could enter the citadel and gain access to all the strategic towers and weaponry that the Drogonians used in the defence of their citadel unnoticed.

Sensing the closeness of the Freelanders and knowing their intentions, Rose again called upon the winds to pick up the invisi-bubbles and bring them into the Citadel itself! Then waiting for just the right moment Rose reached inside herself, turned the hourglass and teleported into the heavily guarded throne room!

Those that had gathered in the courtyard were surprised to see the dragon suddenly disappear but even more surprised to see Freelanders mysteriously appear out of nowhere and stand in the place that the Crimson Dragon had vacated!

Everywhere Freelanders appeared seemingly out of nowhere and held the Drogonians captive with little to no effort! The Drogonians at first surprised and then annoyed with themselves waited for their promised delivery by the

'Crimson Dragon', which as you and I both know would never happen!

Inside the throne room the delighted Drogonian ruler witnessed the appearance of the Crimson Dragon as prophesied! Unaware of the drama taking place both inside and outside the citadel he invited the dragon to approach the throne! Rose noticed that he was quite heavily guarded and knew that it would take more than just her to capture this ruler!

As if by magic; at this precise moment Fidel with Salome brandishing a flaming sword flew through the huge window followed closely by Valour astride Lillie! Unconcerned the Drogonian looked towards the Crimson Dragon to save him! It was then that Rose gave herself a mighty shake; the kind that you see dogs do when they've been for a swim and want to dry themselves! The dried and caked mud fell from the dragon's scales and revealed the true identity of the crimson dragon! Not crimson but red! The Drogonian kingdoms enemy!

The Drogonian king jumped up to run, but it was too late! His guards were now held prisoner by Valour, Salome, Fidel and Lillie! The king had no place to go, he was trapped, as all the exits were blocked by newly arrived and strategically placed Freelander soldiers!

King Luthian's dream of a victory without blood shed had been achieved! There would definitely be celebrations tonight!

# A Victoriuos Return

As you already know, King Luthian was a good, kind and generous king. He wanted all the inhabitants of Freeland to be able to live without arguing and fighting, side by side. He had been relieved by the news that his brother Kyron had not been involved in the revolution, but was puzzled and saddened by his mysterious disappearance during the infiltration and subsequent capture of the Dark Citadel and the defeat of the Drogonian monarchy!

All captives were brought to the Freeland Citadel and taken to see the King. None of the prisoners were able to shed light on the disappearance of Kyron, but were very quick to swear their allegiance to Luthian the Summoner of Light! However, as kind as Luthian was, he was no fool and he therefore made arrangements for all the Drogonians and their followers to be permanently stripped of their powers. He did this by calling upon the help of the time lords.

The time lords who had not taken any part in the battle were asked to help! It was a clever idea......because as you and I know, if you can control time it is very easy to go back to the beginning. And that is exactly what happened! It was as though the Drogonians had never been given powers, special privileges or free will!

No longer would Freeland be terrorized by corrupt citizens and threats of violence. This would be a safe haven for all those that lived or visited! Now the only thing that Freeland needed was time to heal and this they had plenty of! Once again the time lords help was enlisted; they were asked to erase the damage that had been wrought during those terrible years of destruction and all was put right again! As it had been in the beginning! No longer would the trees roam bare and the leaf creatures forced to harvest them for fuel under the watchful eyes of their 'Drogonian keepers.'

The Victory party was now in full swing. Rose, Frank and Vicky were the guests of honour. Later while reminiscing about their adventure they agreed that it was the best time they had had in their entire life, but honestly did not understand all the fuss, as it had been such a sure and easy victory they were convinced it could have been done without them!

The table was a keen point of interest and discussion for those that had never seen it magically materialize all the desired food and drinks! Everyone was invited to the feast without exception, even the now changed Drogonians!

When dusk finally arrived, Luthian excused himself from all the revelry, went outside and awaited the return of the sun to its resting place. Altogether it had been a most successful day and he felt younger than he had done in years!

# Back To Normal

The Drogonians were allowed to return to their homes, barring for the ones that they had forcibly occupied. Bling and his family were once again re-instated in Moth Hall and messengers were sent far and wide to discover the whereabouts of his one missing brother Bliss.

The Dark Citadel was no longer the place that it had been. In fact it was now the resting place of the Moon! For her bravery and part in the war, Salome was awarded the honour of keeper of the Moon; and sometimes on a very clear night; if you look very carefully you will be able to see Fidel's shadow reflected in the moon!

Valour remained in Luthian's service and was given the task to escort Rose, Frank and Vicky home, with the magic of Lillie.

"I will miss you Luthian!"

"And I you Rose, but there comes a time that all good friends must part, each taking a little of the person that they are leaving behind. I will always remember your eagerness and willingness to assist no matter how big the problem may be."

"I will always remember your kindness and patience.......it is these qualities that I take back with me, thank you Luthian."

Vicky suddenly excused herself for she had spotted her tutor and companion, Magpop the dwarf.

"Magpop, you grumpy old thing, I shall miss you!"

"MMMph , ur..........and I you!"

were taught to all the officers in charge of the common Drogonian soldiers. They used this knowledge to enslave and entrap the innocent and now I believe they have taken their skills above earth. Is this true?"

"Unfortunately yes; there has been some evidence of this." answered Bling, hoping that Kyron would continue his tale of how he had landed up as the Drogonian's prisoner and no longer their master!

Kyron was quiet for some time, carefully considering this information, before continuing his story.

"I was afraid that one day this would happen. My only surprise is that it has happened so soon! I thought it would be many more years before the Drogonians discovered another world above ours! I am truly sorry that this has happened and believe me if I could undo any of it I certainly would!"

It was at this point in the tale that Bling noticed Kyron staring at the wall opposite him. If Bling had possessed hair at the back of his neck, it would have been at this point that they would have stood up! Shifting his gaze from Kyron to the wall directly behind him; Bling did not know what to expect or what it was that he might see! All he knew was that suddenly he felt very trapped and if he could he would have fled from that room in that instance never to return!

# Escape From Captivity!

Both Kyron and Bling were now staring at the wall which began to shimmer and slowly disappear! Bling felt his heart leap and jump wildly in fear and dread! The atmosphere in the room was now tense with dreaded expectation.

"You! What are you doing here?" roared the massive Drogonian standing in the space where once a wall had stood. "Why aren't you in the kitchens?"

Bling could not believe his luck! This fierce looking Drogonian had mistaken him for his father! "I, I ........"

"Leave us at once!"

Bling needed no further invitation to leave the room! He scuttled past the huge bear-like creature without a backward glance and found himself in a long corridor with heavy closed doors on either side; leading to two flights of stairs that branched off in two different directions. Confused and unsure which flight of stairs to take, he hesitated for a millisecond and then decided to try going down the flight of stairs on his left hand side. As he approached the staircase he noticed that it had a well polished and smooth banister. As quick as a wink he jumped astride the banister. Facing the corridor and using the wall to push against, he flew down the banister lickety, split!

Thud! Thump! Bump! Ouch! Bling found himself in a heap on the floor of a huge, deserted and empty entrance hall. Picking himself up from the floor and rubbing his bottom, he took stock of himself and his surroundings.

The round entrance hall had one main door leading from it and several smaller doors. In addition to the doors there were several round windows placed at different heights around the room! This architectural oddity proved to be ideal for Bling to see where he was! Standing on his toes and steadying himself with his hands; he was able to reach and look through the lower windows!

To his surprise and delight he was just in time to see Apophis and the 'Crimson' dragon land in the courtyard! No wonder the corridors, stairwells and entrance halls were so deserted! Everyone was outside watching the arrival of the 'Crimson' dragon and Apophis, which was very fortunate for Bling as he could now make his escape without anyone knowing or raising the alarm!

Turning himself invisible, Bling headed towards the main door hoping that he would be able to open it without too much difficulty. Much to his surprise the door was standing slightly ajar and he was able to slip out without been noticed!

Once inside the courtyard Bling cautiously made his way to the drawbridge which had been left unmanned and lowered in the excitement! Thankful for his good fortune Bling made his way quickly and quietly out of the Citadel and towards the surrounding forest where King Luthian's army were waiting for word from the Dark Citadel.

Although he was still invisible, Bling's arrival in the forest did not go unnoticed by the sentry who was on duty.

"Halt! Who goes there?"

Making himself visible and facing the direction from where he had heard the voice coming from, Bling introduced himself.

Stepping out from behind a huge oak tree where he had concealed himself, the sentry smiled and welcomed Bling. "Come, the commander has been expecting your arrival."

Feeling very important and proud of himself, Bling followed the sentry who was making his way further into the forest towards a small clearing surrounded by a ring of ancient and gnarled oak trees who were in what appeared to be a deep conversation with the commander and the Crystal Dragon.

# Reporting To The Commander

Bling carefully picked his way through the dense undergrowth of the forest, following in the footsteps of the sentry who was trying hard not to walk too quickly in his excitement!

"Sir may I interrupt you to announce the arrival of Bling,"

Frank, the Crystal Dragon and the trees all stopped in mid-conversation, to welcome Bling back from his dangerous spying mission.

"Well Bling, you little rascal, you managed to get in and out of the Citadel without raising any alarms. Well done! I am really pleased with you!"

A hush now fell in the open glade as everyone waited expectantly for Bling to speak.

"Thank you sir, I am pleased to have been of service to you. I do have some very good but surprising news for the king"

"Anything you tell me will be available to the king immediately", assured Frank.

"Well sir, as I entered into the Citadel, I noticed a creature carrying food. I felt compelled to follow this creature that was making his way towards the dungeons of the citadel............"

Bling was thoroughly enjoying himself in the retelling of his heroic deeds, pausing every now and then for dramatic effect!

Soon Bling had attracted a huge audience and he was pleased to note that Blog was one of those who had come to listen to his great tale of escape!

As Bling's tale was coming to a close and he had reached the point in his story where he had been mistaken for his father, Blog squealed with delight! Like Bling he had been unaware of what had happened to his family and had assumed the worse, supposing all of them to have been captured and tortured to death! This indeed was good news and he could hardly wait to speak to Bling in private so they could celebrate this good news!

As the tale came to an end; Frank became deep in thought. Like Bling he was both surprised by the capture of Kyron but concerned whether Kyron could be trusted as an ally!

Bling took this moment of deep contemplation as a sign that his company was no longer required and both he and Blog slipped out of the clearing almost unnoticed!

# CHAPTER 8

## Army On The Move

On hearing that the drawbridge was unmanned and unguarded Frank took the decision to mobilise the armed forces immediately!  An opportunity like this was not an opportunity to be missed; he had to act very quickly!

The call to arms was sounded and like a well oiled machine the soldiers filed into their ranks without a whisper; expectantly, waiting for their commander to give them their marching orders.

Flanked by the Crystal Dragon and Salome astride Fidel, Frank and Valour turned towards this brave and trusting army.

"Today we fight for truth and freedom!  May the sun be behind you and the wind in front, let us catch this fish while the water is disturbed!"

This may seem like a strange thing to say to an army going into battle, but Frank knew if the enemy's attention was elsewhere they would not be expecting an attack! Further more he could see that the sun was in an advantageous position for the army as it would mean that the enemy would have to look into the sun in order to fight them; this would give the Freelanders another advantage! Every thing now depended on the ability of the Freelander army to secure the occupation of the citadel with as little bloodshed as possible! Once again they were to make use of the invisi-bubbles so that they could enter the citadel and gain access to all the strategic towers and weaponry that the Drogonians used in the defence of their citadel unnoticed.

Sensing the closeness of the Freelanders and knowing their intentions, Rose again called upon the winds to pick up the invisi-bubbles and bring them into the Citadel itself! Then waiting for just the right moment Rose reached inside herself, turned the hourglass and teleported into the heavily guarded throne room!

Those that had gathered in the courtyard were surprised to see the dragon suddenly disappear but even more surprised to see Freelanders mysteriously appear out of nowhere and stand in the place that the Crimson Dragon had vacated!

Everywhere Freelanders appeared seemingly out of nowhere and held the Drogonians captive with little to no effort! The Drogonians at first surprised and then annoyed with themselves waited for their promised delivery by the

'Crimson Dragon', which as you and I both know would never happen!

Inside the throne room the delighted Drogonian ruler witnessed the appearance of the Crimson Dragon as prophesied! Unaware of the drama taking place both inside and outside the citadel he invited the dragon to approach the throne! Rose noticed that he was quite heavily guarded and knew that it would take more than just her to capture this ruler!

As if by magic; at this precise moment Fidel with Salome brandishing a flaming sword flew through the huge window followed closely by Valour astride Lillie! Unconcerned the Drogonian looked towards the Crimson Dragon to save him! It was then that Rose gave herself a mighty shake; the kind that you see dogs do when they've been for a swim and want to dry themselves! The dried and caked mud fell from the dragon's scales and revealed the true identity of the crimson dragon! Not crimson but red! The Drogonian kingdoms enemy!

The Drogonian king jumped up to run, but it was too late! His guards were now held prisoner by Valour, Salome, Fidel and Lillie! The king had no place to go, he was trapped, as all the exits were blocked by newly arrived and strategically placed Freelander soldiers!

King Luthian's dream of a victory without blood shed had been achieved! There would definitely be celebrations tonight!

# A Victoriuos Return

As you already know, King Luthian was a good, kind and generous king. He wanted all the inhabitants of Freeland to be able to live without arguing and fighting, side by side. He had been relieved by the news that his brother Kyron had not been involved in the revolution, but was puzzled and saddened by his mysterious disappearance during the infiltration and subsequent capture of the Dark Citadel and the defeat of the Drogonian monarchy!

All captives were brought to the Freeland Citadel and taken to see the King. None of the prisoners were able to shed light on the disappearance of Kyron, but were very quick to swear their allegiance to Luthian the Summoner of Light! However, as kind as Luthian was, he was no fool and he therefore made arrangements for all the Drogonians and their followers to be permanently stripped of their powers. He did this by calling upon the help of the time lords.

The time lords who had not taken any part in the battle were asked to help! It was a clever idea......because as you and I know, if you can control time it is very easy to go back to the beginning. And that is exactly what happened! It was as though the Drogonians had never been given powers, special privileges or free will!

No longer would Freeland be terrorized by corrupt citizens and threats of violence. This would be a safe haven for all those that lived or visited! Now the only thing that Freeland needed was time to heal and this they had plenty of! Once again the time lords help was enlisted; they were asked to erase the damage that had been wrought during those terrible years of destruction and all was put right again! As it had been in the beginning! No longer would the trees roam bare and the leaf creatures forced to harvest them for fuel under the watchful eyes of their 'Drogonian keepers.'

The Victory party was now in full swing. Rose, Frank and Vicky were the guests of honour. Later while reminiscing about their adventure they agreed that it was the best time they had had in their entire life, but honestly did not understand all the fuss, as it had been such a sure and easy victory they were convinced it could have been done without them!

The table was a keen point of interest and discussion for those that had never seen it magically materialize all the desired food and drinks! Everyone was invited to the feast without exception, even the now changed Drogonians!

When dusk finally arrived, Luthian excused himself from all the revelry, went outside and awaited the return of the sun to its resting place. Altogether it had been a most successful day and he felt younger than he had done in years!

# Back To Normal

The Drogonians were allowed to return to their homes, barring for the ones that they had forcibly occupied. Bling and his family were once again re-instated in Moth Hall and messengers were sent far and wide to discover the whereabouts of his one missing brother Bliss.

The Dark Citadel was no longer the place that it had been. In fact it was now the resting place of the Moon! For her bravery and part in the war, Salome was awarded the honour of keeper of the Moon; and sometimes on a very clear night; if you look very carefully you will be able to see Fidel's shadow reflected in the moon!

Valour remained in Luthian's service and was given the task to escort Rose, Frank and Vicky home, with the magic of Lillie.

"I will miss you Luthian!"

"And I you Rose, but there comes a time that all good friends must part, each taking a little of the person that they are leaving behind. I will always remember your eagerness and willingness to assist no matter how big the problem may be."

"I will always remember your kindness and patience.......it is these qualities that I take back with me, thank you Luthian."

Vicky suddenly excused herself for she had spotted her tutor and companion, Magpop the dwarf.

"Magpop, you grumpy old thing, I shall miss you!"

"MMMph , ur..........and I you!"

Everyone started to laugh, because this was about as much emotion and feeling that Magpop had ever admitted to in his whole life! He then turned beetroot red and excused himself; but all who saw him later swore that they were sure that they'd seen him wipe a tear from his eye.

Frank was now looking forward to returning home as he had run out of tea that morning and this was one thing the magic table had trouble materializing! And as you and I both know Frank relied on his morning tea to start the day!

Rose was curious as to why Luthian had asked Valour and Lillie to escort them back home as she thought they were going to use the trunkulator!

"Unfortunately, while you have been away, someone took an axe and then set fire to the nut tree, so it is no more," explained Luthian.

The family were shocked by this news and hoped that their home had not been vandalized by the same thugs that had chopped down and set the nut tree alight!

Anxious to get home now, they dilly dallied no more and quicker than you can say "Geronimo", Lillie sprinkled pink dust and they found themselves at home once more!

Frank put the kettle on while Rose ran out into the garden to see what damaged had been done to the tree! To her disappointment it had been completely destroyed and any hopes of trying to salvage it were dashed! This meant that she would never be able to travel to Freeland again and visit her new found friends! It was while she was outside contemplating her bad luck when the neighbour arrived and told her the full story of what had happened to the nut tree and how the fire department had tried to put out the flames!

# The Nut Tree Saga

The kettle had boiled and Frank had made four cups of steaming hot tea. With Vicky's help he carried the cups of the aromatic, steaming hot drink to the two ladies standing where once the nut tree had been! Rose and the neighbour were discussing what had happened on the night that the tree had been set alight!

"Ta, nothing like a cup of Frank's tea, is what I always say," said the neighbour and then she began to tell the story.

"I woke up at about 11 o'clock, 'cos I heard the dogs barking and I looked out the window, but couldn't see nothing. I was about to go back to bed when a slight movement caught my attention from the corner of my eye! I thought I must have been dreaming 'cos I swear I saw what looked like a bear and an old man step out from the ground in front of the tree! Naturally I rubbed my eyes and pinched my arm just to make sure I was awake, and lo and behold there was the two of them still, chopping away at the tree with what looked like an axe to me!

Straight away I tried to phone the 'coppers' 'cos I couldn't see lights on in your place and guessed that you wasn't in but the phone didn't want to work! It was completely dead! So I ran outside to chase them away, but then I....I couldn't move! You ever play stuck- in- the mud as kids? Well this was like that, 'cept I was stuck for real!

I tried to call for help, but I couldn't make a sound....... my voice just wouldn't come out of my mouth and no matter how hard I was screaming in my head, not a sound came out!

Rose, Frank and Vicky couldn't help but admire the bravery of this woman and were shocked to discover that during the occupation of the Dark Citadel, a Drogonian and one other had managed to escape using the trunkulator! There was no way of getting this news to Luthian!

"Well, then I must of fallen asleep, outside in my backyard...'cos I don't remember another thing! All I remember is waking up, seeing the fire ..........and phoning the fire brigade, 'cos now my phone was working! Even though the fire engine arrived very quickly they couldn't save the tree! All they managed to do was keep the fire from spreading 'cos that fire was so hot nothing could put it out. Then a curious thing happened......as if by magic.......the fire suddenly stopped and the only thing that had actually burnt was the tree itself, anything near wasn't even scorched by the blaze! Very strange don't you think?"

The family agreed with the neighbour and thanked her for all that she had done, but they didn't dare tell her that it probably was a magical fire, because they had sworn a secrecy oath to tell no-one about Freeland!

That day was spent like any other, except for the picking up of all the charred wood bits and throwing them away!

Vicky secretly kept one small piece of wood and put it in her secret place as a reminder of her adventures in 'another place!'

# Vicky's Thoughts

"I'm bored already! I wish that I could go off on another adventure!"

Mum always told me that you must be careful of what you wish for because they have a funny way of coming true!

I would never have guessed how close I was to getting this wish!

But that is another story and I need to tidy my room before I get into trouble for leaving it in such a mess!

THE END

Lightning Source UK Ltd.
Milton Keynes UK
UKOW04f1907180917
309431UK00001B/4/P